Magic Ponies

Riding Rescue

To Strawberry, pretty funster with attitude—SB

GROSSET & DUNLAP
Published by the Penguin Group
Penguin Group (USA) Inc., 375 Hudson Street, New York, New York 10014, USA

USA | Canada | UK | Ireland | Australia | New Zealand | India | South Africa | China
Penguin Books Ltd, Registered Offices: 80 Strand, London WC2R 0RL, England

For more information about the Penguin Group visit penguin.com

Text copyright © 2009 by Sue Bentley. Illustrations copyright © 2009 by Angela Swan. Cover illustration © 2009 by Andrew Farley. First printed in Great Britain in 2009 by Penguin Books Ltd. First published in the United States in 2013 by Grosset & Dunlap, a division of Penguin Young Readers Group, 345 Hudson Street, New York, New York 10014. GROSSET & DUNLAP is a trademark of Penguin Group (USA) Inc. Printed in the U.S.A.

Library of Congress Cataloging-in-Publication Data is available.

ISBN 978-0-448-46735-1   10 9 8 7 6 5 4 3

Magic Ponies

Riding Rescue

SUE BENTLEY

illustrated by Angela Swan

Grosset & Dunlap
An Imprint of Penguin Group (USA) Inc.

Prologue

Comet spread his gold-feathered wings as he glided above Rainbow Mist Island. Below him, the magic pony could see the tiny figures of pale horses with sparkling golden wings galloping toward a deep valley.

Lightning Horses—members of his own herd! Comet wondered if one of them could be Destiny, his long-lost twin sister.

Circling lower, he soared downward to land and felt the velvety grass beneath his shining hooves. It felt good to be home.

As the magic pony galloped along, sunlight flashed on his cream-colored coat and gold mane and tail. Through a gap in the rocks, he saw a waterfall gushing into a deep clear pool. Perhaps Destiny and the other Lightning Horses were making their way there to drink.

Checking his stride, Comet picked his way across big slabs of rock toward the tumbling water. Pastel-colored ferns grew among a carpet of silver and gold flowers. Everything was wreathed in the fine multicolored mist that gave Rainbow Mist Island its name.

Comet sensed a movement in some nearby birch trees, and his lonely heart lifted with hope.

"Destiny!"

A pale-cream horse with a wise expression stepped out. "I am afraid she is not here. But it is good to see you again, my young friend," he said in a deep musical whinny.

"Blaze!" Comet tried to hide his disappointment as he bent his head before the leader of the Lightning Herd. "I hoped Destiny had come back."

Blaze's gold eyes softened. "I do not think she will return while she believes she is in trouble for losing our stone."

The Stone of Power protected the herd from the dark horses who wanted to steal their power. It had been lost during their game of cloud-chasing. Comet had found the stone, but his twin sister had already fled.

"I can hardly bear to think of her being so far away and all alone," Comet said sadly. "Where can she be?"

"The stone will help us find her." Blaze stamped his front hoof on the grass and a gleaming fiery opal appeared, shining with multicolored light. "Come closer. Look into the stone."

As Comet did so, the stone grew in size and became brighter and brighter. An image appeared in its glittering depths. Comet saw Destiny cantering across a hillside in a world far away.

"I must go to her!" he cried.

There was a bright flash of violet light, and glittering rainbow mist swirled all around him. The young cream-colored pony with gold-feathered wings and a gold mane and tail disappeared, and in its place stood a sturdy Dartmoor pony, with a glossy bay coat, a paler sandy muzzle, and a chocolate-brown mane and tail.

"Go now. Use this disguise and search for Destiny. Find her before the dark horses discover her," Blaze neighed.

Comet nodded. "I will bring her back safely!" he vowed.

A soft neigh rumbled from him, and violet sparks glinted in his bay coat. Rainbow mist thickened and began swirling around him as it drew him in.

Chapter
ONE

Gina Carey smiled nervously up at the young nurse who was about to remove the plaster cast on her arm. "Will it hurt?" Gina asked her.

"You won't feel a thing, I promise!" the nurse said reassuringly.

"Really?" Gina said doubtfully. She was a real wimp when it came to anything to do with doctors and hospitals.

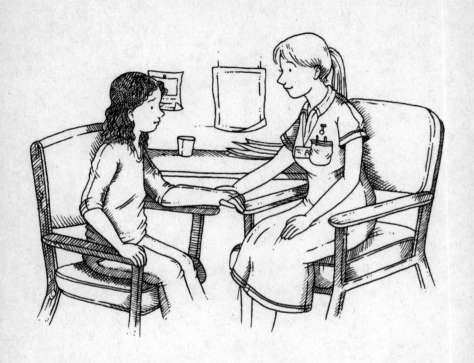

As the nurse got to work, there was a
whiny whirring noise. Mrs. Carey stood
nearby. She smiled at Gina. Moments
later, the cast fell into pieces and the nurse
removed it.

Gina grinned. "Cool! It didn't even
tickle!"

"Told you!" the nurse said, grinning.
"There, all done!"

"You'll be riding again in no time, honey," Mrs. Carey said.

"I hope so." Gina tried not to think about the riding accident in which she had broken her arm. She swallowed hard, determined not to get upset in front of the nurse.

Luckily, her mom was already gathering up her schoolbag. There was a line of people waiting for treatment at the clinic, so Gina and her mom quickly thanked the nurse and headed for the parking lot.

"Now that school is over for a few weeks, are you looking forward to summer camp with Katie and Lewis?" Mrs. Carey asked as she drove home.

Katie and Lewis were Gina's best friends. They all went to Pony Club together.

"Mmm—yeah," Gina murmured. She stared out the side window for the rest of the short drive home.

The phone was ringing in the hall as they walked through the front door, and Gina hurried inside to answer it. It was Lewis, asking if she'd had her cast removed.

"Yep! Piece of cake!" Gina told him, leaving out the part about the butterflies in her tummy before it came off. "My arm's all healed. It feels fine now."

"Cool! So—are you packed and ready?" he asked. "Dad's giving us all a lift. It's going to be amazing. Nothing to do all day but riding and pony stuff! I hope I don't get saddle sore!" he joked.

"Um . . . me too," Gina said quickly.

"See you later. Bye."

After Lewis hung up, she stood in the hall, deep in thought. Who was she kidding? Since the accident, she'd felt nervous at the mere thought of getting back onto a pony. She hadn't told anyone about this, hoping that she'd feel better by the time she went to summer camp.

Her mom was moving around the kitchen making lunch. Gina sighed heavily as she hovered in the doorway. She didn't hear her dad come out of his office and almost jumped out of her skin when he touched her shoulder.

"You look a bit pale, Gina. Are you feeling okay?" Mr. Carey asked.

"Yes. No. Not really. I . . . I . . ." To Gina's dismay, her eyes filled with tears and it all came pouring out. How she couldn't stop thinking about the accident and what had happened to River, her gentle gray pony. And how the very thought of riding sent her into a complete panic. "I can't face going to camp! But I'll be letting Lewis and Katie down if I don't go," she wailed.

"Oh, sweetheart!" Mrs. Carey came over to give her a hug. "You should have said so earlier. You're still hurting after losing River. Katie and Lewis will

understand. I'll call their parents right
away and explain that you're going to skip
out on camp this time."

"Thanks, Mom." Gina gulped, feeling
relieved.

Her mom went into the hall and
returned a few minutes later. "There.
That's settled. No problem. Everyone
was fine with it," Mrs. Carey said gently,
smiling.

Gina's dad reached out to pat Gina's
arm. "Don't be too hard on yourself,
honey. It takes time to get over a shock.
You'll ride again when you're ready."

But I won't be riding River, Gina
thought sadly. Her plucky little pony's
injuries had been serious. She had gone to
live in an animal park and would never be
ridden again.

Gina forced herself to be brave as she tucked a strand of her dark hair behind her ears. She gave her mom and dad a weak smile, glad that they were being so nice and understanding.

"Now that you have time on your hands, how about coming with me to Horseland?" her mom suggested after a while. "Angie will appreciate some extra help."

Angie Blackwell, a close family friend, had recently set up a horse and pony rescue center. Gina's mom lent a hand whenever she could.

"Okay. As long as I don't have to ride any of the ponies," Gina said. She'd been itching to see how Horseland was coming along. The regular reports she'd been getting from her mom sounded great.

"You'll more likely be mucking out stables and cleaning tack," Mrs. Carey said, gathering the empty plates. "Why don't you go get changed, and I'll meet you at the car."

"Okay." Gina took a deep breath. She was feeling a bit better. "See you later, Dad," she called, running upstairs to get her jeans and boots.

It was only a five-minute car ride to the old farm. A big sign outside read: HORSELAND. A SAFE HAVEN. A NEW START.

Gina loved the message on the sign, which offered hope to the rescued ponies.

They drove up the road to a large stone farmhouse. Gina was impressed. Angie had worked wonders with the place. The old outbuildings had become a stable block, tack room, and storeroom. Orange marigolds and blue pansies glowed from the many tubs and window boxes.

They found Angie in her office, which overlooked the spacious yard. She was puzzling over a computer and looked up with a warm smile to greet Gina's mom. "Hi again, Val. Nice to see you, too, Gina. Come to see how we're doing, have you?"

Gina nodded. "It's looking fantastic. Even better than I'd imagined."

"It's been hard work. But it's a real labor of love." Angie looked pleased. She had a friendly, open face and clear bright-blue eyes. Her shoulder-length fair hair was tied back in a ponytail. "Why don't you have a look around while I convince your mom to help me sort out this database?"

"Okay. See you both later."

Gina went into the yard and made
her way toward the paddock, where
some ponies were enjoying the sunshine.
Whatever condition they had once been
in, they all looked glossy and healthy now.
She stepped onto the bottom bar of the
ranch-style fence and folded her arms on
the top. "Hi, ponies. Who wants to come
and say hello?" she invited.

One or two of them turned curious
heads toward her.

A strange mist, twinkling with glittering rainbow sparkles, hung over the bottom of the paddock.

What a pretty trick of the sunlight, Gina thought. Just then a cute bay Dartmoor pony, with a chocolate-brown mane and tail and a sandy muzzle, stepped out of the mist and walked toward the fence.

"Hello, gorgeous." Gina held out her hand so the bay pony could get her scent.

Twitching its ears forward inquisitively, the Dartmoor pony looked at her. "Can you help me, please?" it asked in a velvety neigh.

Chapter
TWO

Gina pulled her hand back. Her eyes widened as she almost fell backward off the fence in shock. Was this some kind of a joke? She glanced around to see if someone was hiding nearby and playing a trick on her.

But her mom and Angie were still in the office, and the rest of the staff must be inside the stables.

I must be hearing things. Ponies can't talk—not even rescued ones! Gina shook her head slowly. "I wonder where you came from," she said aloud.

"I came from far away. I am Comet of the Lightning Herd, and I am here looking for my twin sister," the Dartmoor pony said, looking at her with big deep-violet eyes.

"You . . . you really can talk!" Gina gasped, still not actually believing this was happening. "How?"

"All the Lightning Horses can talk," Comet explained. "What is your name?"

He was looking at her steadily as if he was expecting an answer. Gina found herself stammering, "G-Gina Carey. I'm . . . h-here with my mom to help . . . with the rescued horses. Mom's friend

Angie runs Horseland."

"I am honored to meet you, Gina."
Comet dipped his head politely.

"Um . . . me too," Gina said. She
remembered something he had said. "Did
you say something about a twin sister? Is
she here, too?"

"No. Destiny is hiding somewhere
nearby," Comet said, his voice softening.

"She ran away after she lost the Stone of Power, when we were cloud-racing. The stone protects us from the dark horses who want to steal our magic. I found it and it is safe again, but Destiny does not know this. She thinks she is in trouble, so she ran away to hide in your world."

Gina was having trouble taking this in. It all sounded so strange, like something out of a fairy tale. "You say that you and your twin sister were cloud-racing—in the sky? But how can—"

Comet tossed his chocolate-brown mane and backed away from the fence. "I will show you," he whinnied gently.

Gina felt a strange warm tingling sensation flowing toward her fingertips as violet sparks glinted in Comet's glossy

bay coat, and another wash of shimmering
rainbow mist swirled around him.

Gina narrowed her eyes, trying to
see through the mist. Then her mouth
fell open as she saw that the Dartmoor
pony had gone, and in its place stood a
magnificent cream-colored pony with
a noble arched neck and a flowing gold
mane and tail. But even more amazing

were the gold-feathered wings that sprang from his shoulders.

"Oh!" Gina gasped, totally spellbound. She had never seen anything so beautiful in her entire life. "Comet?"

"Yes, it is still me," Comet said in a deep musical neigh.

But before Gina could get used to the dazzling sight of Comet in his true form, there was a final swoosh of the glittering rainbow mist, and Comet reappeared as a strongly built Dartmoor pony.

"Wow!" Gina let out a long breath. "That's an amazing disguise! Can Destiny use her magic to do that, too?"

Comet nodded. "But that will not help her if the dark horses discover her. Without the stone's protection, they will see through her magic. I must find her and take her back safely to our home on Rainbow Mist Island. Will you help me, Gina?"

The magic pony's eyes twinkled hopefully, and Gina's soft heart melted as she guessed he was missing his twin. "Of course I will. Wait until Mom and Angie hear about this—"

"No! I am sorry, Gina, but you can tell no one about me or what I have told you!"

Gina hesitated, wishing that she could share this amazing news. Her mom and Angie would have been delighted to think they had rescued a magic pony, and she was sure they would keep Comet's secret.

"You must promise me," Comet insisted gently.

Gina came to a decision. She might not have been able to save River from getting hurt. But she would do anything she could to protect Comet and Destiny from their enemies.

"All right. Cross my heart. Your secret's safe with me."

Comet's large intelligent eyes glowed softly like amethysts. "Thank you, Gina." He gave a soft blow and reached forward to nudge gently against her arm.

Gina stroked his velvety nose, which was a paler sandy color than the rest of him. She breathed in his clean warm smell of grass and apples.

"Soon we will ride out and look for Destiny," he breathed happily, his eyes closed in contentment.

"Um . . . yes. We will," Gina said. To her dismay, she felt a familiar pang of anxiety at the thought of getting back into the saddle.

She felt proud that a magic pony had chosen her to be his special friend. There was no way she was going to let him down. Somehow she would find a way to keep her promise to him.

Chapter
THREE

"There you are, Gina!" Angie cried,
striding toward the paddock. "I've left
your mom battling with the database. She's
a computer whiz. Not like me! It looks
like you've already made a friend."

Gina smiled at Angie. "I have! Comet's
totally gorgeous, isn't he?" she said
without thinking.

Angie looked surprised. "Comet, eh?

It suits him. We haven't come up with a name for this little bay yet, so I think we'll keep that one. He arrived in a truck a couple of days ago, along with some other ponies, but no one seemed to know much about him. Beats me how someone could just abandon a perfectly healthy young pony."

"I know. I really hate people who do stuff like that," Gina agreed with feeling. Of course, Comet hadn't actually been abandoned, but Gina knew that lots of ponies were. Thank goodness for places like Horseland.

Angie patted Comet's silky neck. "Well, you two have certainly cozied up together. Comet didn't happen to tell you where he came from, did he, Gina?" she joked.

"As if!" Gina said, biting back a grin. *If only you knew!* she thought.

Angie turned at the sound of an engine and Gina saw a minibus driving up the road. "It looks like the kids have arrived," Angie commented.

"Kids?" Gina said, puzzled.

"From a local children's center. These kids wouldn't usually get a chance to meet ponies. But here they can interact with them and even ride if they feel

confident enough. After what some of
our ponies have been through, they find it
less threatening to be around youngsters.
It gets them back to feeling comfortable
with adult riders."

Gina thought this was a great idea. She
wondered what it would take to make *her*
feel confident about riding Comet. She
watched as the adults began helping some
of the kids who were in specially adapted
wheelchairs get off the bus as the others
jumped off eagerly around them.

"Minky, especially, enjoys these
sessions. That's him over there." Angie
pointed to a small black-and-white pony
with a kindly expression, which one of
Horseland's regular staff was now tacking
up.

Angie turned back to Gina. "Comet

seems like a calm, sweet-natured pony. I think we'll see how he handles meeting the kids today. Would you like to help?"

"You bet!" Gina said eagerly. She had been perfectly willing to help muck out stables and clean tack, but this sounded much more fun. "What do I have to do?"

"Bring Comet out and tether him in the yard. You'll find what you need in the tack room. Okay?"

"Will do," Gina said. "Back in a sec, Comet!" she whispered. In a few moments she returned with a head collar and lead rope. "I have to put this stuff on you. Is that okay?"

He nodded. "I know of these straps that ponies wear in your world."

Comet stood quietly while Gina fitted him with the head collar, led him

into the yard, and tethered him beside
Minky. The small black-and-white pony
nickered, and Comet gave an answering
snort. Gina smiled as the two ponies
made friends.

Comet lifted his head, and his
chocolate mane stirred in the breeze.
"This will be fun!" he neighed.

Gina did a double take, amazed that
he'd just spoken to her. "Hush!" she
warned him in a whisper. "Someone will

hear you! You don't want to give yourself away."

"I have used my magic so that only you can hear me," he told her, his deep-violet eyes glinting. "To anyone else I will look and sound like an ordinary pony."

"Really? No problem then," Gina whispered delightedly. Comet was so amazing. She wondered what else he could do.

Angie brought over a girl in a motorized wheelchair, and a woman. Every inch of the wheelchair was covered with bright stickers of bands and singers.

"This is Felicity Norton and Jane, her caretaker. I'll leave them with you and Comet, Gina. Okay?" she said with an encouraging smile. "I'll be just across the yard. Call me if you need me."

"No problem." Gina felt a little nervous, but hoped it didn't show. "Hi, Felicity. I'm Gina Carey," she said, smiling.

"Hi," the girl replied. "You can call me Fliss. Everyone does." She looked about seven years old and had a delicate pale face with big hazel eyes. Her light brown hair was tied in pigtails. She wore pink sneakers, and there was a sparkly star, in matching pink, on the front of her gray tracksuit.

Gina looked questioningly at Jane, Fliss's caretaker.

The woman smiled. "Don't mind me, Gina. I'm just here to help Fliss get in and out of the wheelchair. You two just carry on. Okay?"

"Okay, fine," Gina said. She turned back to Fliss. "This is Comet. He's a sweet, gentle pony."

"He's really *huge!*" Fliss turned to Gina and looked her up and down. "And you don't look much older than me," she said bluntly. "How come you've got a job here?"

Gina grinned. "I'm almost ten, but I guess I look younger. I'm just helping out. Angie knows that I've been around ponies forever. I used to have my own pony called River, but I haven't got her anymore."

"Why not?" Fliss asked.

Gina bit her lip, wishing she hadn't mentioned her. "It's a long story. Maybe I'll tell you some other time. How about you? Do you like ponies, Fliss?" she asked, quickly changing the subject.

"Dunno. Never met one." Fliss shrugged her narrow shoulders.

"Never?" Gina couldn't imagine not having ponies in her life. "Well, now's your chance," she said encouragingly. "You're going to love making friends with Comet!"

Fliss looked a bit nervous as she craned her neck to look up at Comet. "What do I have to do?"

"Well—it's always best to come up to a pony from the side, rather than straight on. He'll see you better that way, and you won't seem so scary to him. Talk to Comet gently and then hold your hand out flat, so he can get your scent. Do you want to try that first and see how you like it?"

"I can do that. It's not exactly rocket science, is it?" Fliss scoffed, her eyes twinkling mischievously. She pressed the controls, and her wheelchair trundled into position.

Gina hid a smile. Fliss was a riot. She wondered what Comet would make of the outspoken little girl.

The magic pony's eyes softened as he leaned down and snuffled Fliss's outstretched palm. "Hello, Fliss. Pleased to meet you," he neighed softly—but of course Fliss heard only normal pony noises. He then gently huffed a warm breath into her hair.

"Oh!" Fliss nearly jumped out of her skin. "That tickles!" she spluttered with delighted laughter. "Why did he do that?"

"It's his way of being friendly," Gina explained. "Comet likes you."

"Really? Cool! I like him, too." Her thin face brightening, she reached up slowly, and tentatively stroked Comet's nose. "Oh, it's lovely—all warm and soft, like velvet!"

Gina beamed as Fliss and Comet got to know each other. Fliss was soon confidently patting him and stroking his cheek. The meeting was a success!

"Maybe you'd like to sit on Comet's back another time?" she suggested. "If that's okay with you?" she said, looking at Jane, who stood nearby.

Fliss's caretaker nodded. "No problem.

I'll help her get up onto the pony, but then she'll be fine."

Fliss looked excited but apprehensive at the idea. "Maybe. I dunno. It's an awful long way up. I'd have to think about it," she said warily.

Angie strolled over. "Well, you seem to be getting along well with Gina and Comet, Felicity. Would you like to meet some of our other ponies?"

"Okay. But Comet's definitely my fave," Fliss said, grinning proudly. "He's totally awesome!"

"I couldn't agree more!" Gina said, smiling as Fliss, Jane, and Angie crossed the yard. "See you again soon!" she called.

"You bet!" Fliss shouted back, wheeling around to give her a thumbs-up. "Bye, Comet. See you next time."

Just then, there was a startled cry from one of the helpers.

Gina saw that a small boy was clinging on tight to Minky's back as the little black-and-white pony pranced around and pulled against its tether.

Angie was trying to calm the agitated pony. "Minky! Stand!" she said firmly. "What's gotten into you?"

Gina frowned. Minky had seemed
so calm and friendly earlier. What could
be wrong? As the pony's eyes rolled and
his hindquarters tightened, she read
the telltale signs. "Oh no!" she gasped.
"Minky's going to buck! That boy will be
thrown off!" Suddenly, she felt a tingling
sensation flowing down to the tips of her
fingers as big violet sparkles ignited in
Comet's bay coat, and tiny rainbow flashes
of magical power rippled through his
chocolate-brown mane and tail.

Something very strange was about to
happen.

Chapter
FOUR

Gina watched in utter amazement as
Comet opened his mouth and breathed
out a long sparkly breath. A cloud
of shimmering multicolored glitter
whooshed across the yard toward Minky.
Gina looked around to see if anyone else
could see the magical rainbow mist, but it
seemed visible only to her.

The glittering particles whirled

around the black-and-white pony for a few
seconds, making it look as if Minky stood
in the center of a snow globe. Then the
sparkles faded away into rainbow dust and
disappeared, along with every last violet
spark.

The panic left the little pony's eyes, and
he grew calm again. Minky stood quietly as
Angie and one of the caretakers helped the
boy get down from the pony and back into
his wheelchair.

Gina could see little tremors flickering
over the pony's black-and-white coat, and he
was twitching his tail in distress. She frowned.
"There's still something wrong with him."

Comet thought so, too. Swiveling his
ears, he whickered to Minky. The little
pony turned his head. Wrinkling his lips, he
nickered back.

Comet listened closely and then
neighed softly to Gina. "Minky has told
me that something is digging into his back
and hurting him."

"Oh, the poor thing. No wonder he
was acting up," Gina said.

She hurried straight over to Angie,

who looked very embarrassed. "Oh dear. I'm so sorry he scared you, Tommy," she apologized to the boy. "Minky's usually so steady and reliable. I don't know what got into him today."

Tommy grinned up at her, his face flushed. "I'm okay! It was almost like being in a rodeo!" he said, looking none the worse for his fright.

"I'm afraid that's not the point, though, Tommy," said the caretaker, a tall young man named Bill. "How do we know that this won't happen again?"

"Well—" Angie began.

"Excuse me, but I've got an idea about what happened," Gina interrupted politely. "Do you mind if I look at Minky's saddle?"

Angie raised her eyebrows in surprise. "Go ahead," she said, looking puzzled.

Gina loosened the girth and removed
Minky's saddle. She ran her fingers under
it, where they immediately snagged
on a small prickly seed head. "Just as I
thought!" She extracted the burr and
showed it to Angie. "This was digging into
Minky's back!"

"So that's why he shied!" Angie patted
Minky's cheek. "Poor boy. You were trying
to tell us you were in pain." She looked at

Gina. "Thanks, Gina. It was very clever of you to work that out," she praised warmly.

Gina smiled. "It wasn't that hard," she said modestly.

She wished she could tell Angie that it was Comet who deserved all the credit, but she would never reveal his secret.

With the mystery solved, Gina left Angie smoothing things over with Tommy and the caretaker. She patted Comet and stroked his thick mane. "Well done, Comet," she whispered, looking at him adoringly. "You were brilliant!"

The magic pony twitched his tail. "I am glad that I could help."

Gina felt a rush of affection for her magical friend. She decided that he deserved a treat. "I'll be right back!" she told him, dashing off toward the stable kitchen in search of an especially juicy, crunchy apple.

✴

"So you enjoyed your first visit to Horseland?" Mrs. Carey asked later as they drove home.

"It was amazing. The rescued ponies are beautiful," Gina said. "It's hard to believe that some of them were once neglected. The ones I met all look like they're in great condition. Minky, the little black-and-white pony, is really cute. And there's Dancer, she's a roan-colored Welsh pony. And Porter is stunning. He's an ex–show jumper. And then there's Comet, the bay Dartmoor pony. He's absolutely gorgeous, the best of all! And—"

"Whoa! Slow down a bit," her mom said, laughing. "I can't keep up!"

Gina grinned. "Sorry. I got a bit carried away. It's a fantastic place. Can I go over there again tomorrow? Angie says I'm welcome anytime."

"Of course you can. Angie was very impressed with you. She told me what happened with Minky. You helped her with what could have been a very difficult situation. Well done, sweetie. I'm very proud of you."

Gina blushed. "Oh, it wasn't much."

"Well, I'm very impressed," her mom said firmly. "And I can see that you've totally fallen in love with that bay. What's his name again?"

"Comet," Gina said. "He's pretty special."

"He certainly seems to have worked some kind of magic on you."

"What . . . what do you mean?" Gina

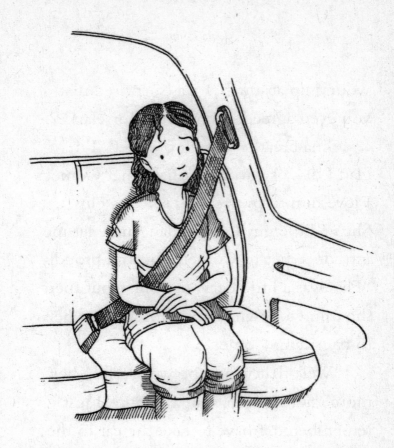

asked nervously. Had her mom heard
her talking to the magic pony? *Please tell
me I haven't given away Comet's secret*, she
thought, her heart thumping.

Mrs. Carey smiled. "I just meant that
you're like a different girl. You were pretty

wound up at lunch. I was surprised that you even agreed to come to Horseland."

Gina breathed a sigh of relief. "I'm glad I did, or I wouldn't have met Comet. I love him to pieces. And so does Fliss. She's a little girl I met today. Angie let me introduce her to Comet," she said proudly. "Fliss was a little nervous at first, but then she calmed down. I think I might get her to try riding Comet."

"Well, that would be wonderful," her mom said. "Oh no, wait a minute. I just remembered. I have to take the car to the garage tomorrow morning, so I can't give you a lift."

"That's okay. I can ride my bike over," Gina said at once.

Her mom's eyes widened in shock. "Since when did you offer to bike anywhere? You really *are* excited to be around those rescued ponies, aren't you? I don't blame you. It's a great feeling when you see the poor things beginning to get their confidence back and learning to trust people again."

Gina nodded. She couldn't agree more. "If only I could get *my* confidence back to start riding again," she murmured wistfully, thinking of helping Comet look for Destiny.

Her mom gave her a knowing grin. "Trust me, honey. Someone as crazy about ponies as you won't be able to resist getting back into the saddle for very much longer!"

Gina smiled and her spirits lifted a little as she hoped her mom was right.

Chapter
FIVE

Gina woke up the next morning to
find the sun shining through her bedroom
curtains. Birds twittered from the nearby
trees, but it was so early that she couldn't
hear any cars going past on the road
outside.

She was eager to see Comet again, if
only to prove that yesterday hadn't been
just an incredible dream. Throwing back

the covers, she shot out of bed and threw
on her shorts and T-shirt. After a hurried
gulp of fruit juice in the kitchen, she left
a note for her mom and dad to tell them
where she'd gone, hopped on her bike,
and set out for Horseland.

It had been ages since Gina had ridden
her bike, and she was puffing hard by the
time she reached the top of the hill above
the old farm. She rested her aching leg
muscles when she coasted down the slope

on the other side and then turned into Horseland's entrance.

Morning mist still covered the grass in the empty paddock, and Gina guessed that all the ponies were still shut up safely in the stable. There was no sign of Angie or any of her staff, so opening the door, she slipped inside.

Comet was looking over his stall and spotted her immediately. He gave a neigh of welcome. "Greetings, Gina!"

"Hi, Comet!" Gina threw her arms around the magic pony's silky neck and pressed her cheek against his warm skin. "I missed you, so I rode my bike over here the moment I got up."

"Thank you for coming here this early," Comet snorted. There was a little flurry of sparks, and the door of his stall

opened. He stepped out to stand beside
her. "Now we have time to go out looking
for Destiny. Please climb onto my back."

Gina froze and her mouth went dry.
Maybe if she just climbed straight up onto
Comet's back, she'd feel okay.

But her legs trembled as she stepped
onto the mounting block. *I have to do this,*
she told herself. With a superhuman effort,
she forced herself to swing her right leg up
and over. Closing her eyes and fighting a
wave of panic, she took a firm hold of his
mane.

"R-ready," she murmured shakily.

Comet didn't move. His ears flattened
and he turned to look at her. "Is something
wrong, Gina? You do not seem happy to
ride me."

Gina swallowed and tears burned her

eyes. "I do want to, more than anything!
But . . . I . . . j-just can't. Not yet!"
She scrambled off his back onto the
mounting block. Once on the ground,
she stood with her head down and her
arms hanging by her sides. "I'm so sorry,
Comet. I've let you down! I wouldn't
blame you if you hated me! You should

find someone else to help you, someone who isn't useless!" she burst out.

She whirled and ran into the stable yard. Tears of humiliation blinded her. She had failed Comet. There was no way she could keep her promise to help him find Destiny.

Suddenly, Comet was walking beside her, his shining hooves making no sound on the ground.

"Please stop, Gina," he neighed softly, turning to look at her with kind eyes. "You must tell me everything."

Gina nodded wretchedly. She took a deep breath and told her magical friend everything. "I . . . I had a bad accident a few months ago. I was in a field, riding my pony, River, when a car backfired nearby and scared her. River reared up, and I fell off and broke my arm. She bolted and caught her foot in a rabbit hole and hurt herself really badly. River almost had to be—" Gina stopped for a moment, unable to say the awful words. "But she got well enough to go and live in an animal park. I lost my beautiful pony. And I've been really scared to ride since then."

Comet nodded slowly and his mane fell forward. "That was a horrible thing to happen. It is very sad to lose a dear friend. On Rainbow Mist Island, we have a saying: 'No one is ever far away when they are in our memories.'"

Gina laid her face against his warm cheek and was surprised to feel her sadness easing a little. "That's true. I think about River every day, and Mom says we

can go and visit her sometime. I know
she would want me to ride again, but
the thought of it still scares me stiff," she
admitted, hanging her head.

Comet was silent for a moment. "I
have an idea," he neighed at last.

"Really?" Gina looked up into
the magic pony's beautiful eyes, which
glowed with affection and understanding.

"Are you going to use your magic to make me forget about what happened and stop me being afraid?" she asked hopefully.

"No, Gina. That would not be right. Our memories are part of who we are. You must find a way to be strong. I will not always be here to solve problems for you."

Gina felt a pang as she realized that one day her friend would have to leave and return to his own world with his twin sister. But she couldn't bear to think of that right now.

"Thank you for being so kind, Comet. You're the best friend ever," she said, holding out her hands.

Comet gently pushed his nose into her cupped palms. She felt his warm breath on her fingers as they shared a moment of closeness she knew she would treasure always.

"Are you going to look for Destiny now?" she asked eventually.

Comet nodded, a gleam of determination in his eyes. "Yes. And you are going to help me!"

"But . . . but . . . how can I?" Gina's heart missed a beat. Was he going to insist that she ride him after all?

Chapter
SIX

Gina gasped as she felt a tingling
sensation flow right down to the ends of
her fingertips. Large violet sparks glowed
in the magic pony's bay coat, and a thick
mist flowed around them, shimmering
and glowing with all the colors of the
rainbow.

She felt something soft and springy
beneath her feet and looked down to see

that she and Comet were standing on a
small, fluffy white cloud.

"Hold tight, Gina!" Comet instructed.

Gina wrapped one hand in his thick
chocolate mane. She felt a surge of
excitement as they rose into the air and
floated across the fields. Suddenly, they
shot forward on the cloud, whizzing

across hills and valleys and zooming along above forests and woods.

Two surprised-looking pigeons fluttered out of a tree as they flew past. A gray squirrel chattered and dived for cover.

"Wow! This is great!" Gina exclaimed as they raced along at almost the speed of light. It was wonderful to be pressed up close against Comet's warm, strong shoulder and feel his glittery magic enfolding her. She felt safe and secure beside him on the pillowy cloud, however high they floated in the air.

They descended once to check out some ponies in a field, but none of them were Destiny. For the rest of their trip, Gina and Comet saw no other ponies.

As Comet's ears flattened with disappointment, Gina stroked his satiny neck. "We'll find her. We'll keep on looking until we do," she promised. "You never know, she might already have come past this way."

"No, she has not, Gina. Or she would have left a trail," Comet told her.

Gina was intrigued. "What sort of trail?"

"A line of softly glowing hoofprints. Not many people in your world can see them."

"Will I be able to?" Gina asked.

Comet nodded. "Yes, if you are riding me or if we are very close." He looked up at the sky, where the sun was now above the trees. "We must return to Horseland— they will be wondering where you are."

Gina clung on tight to his mane as the cloud whooshed back through the clear morning air above the treetops. A patchwork of fields rushed past below them, along with miniature villages and roads with toy cars and houses. In no time at all they were hovering over the familiar farmhouse and stable yard.

There was a final violet flash and a burst of rainbow sparkles, and Gina found herself back on solid ground, standing inside the stable in front of Comet's stall. It wasn't a moment too soon.

Angie Blackwell came in, pushing a wheelbarrow. "So it's your bike outside! That solves the mystery," she said with a broad grin. "You're an early bird this morning."

Gina grinned. "I know. I just couldn't keep away."

"Come to see Comet again, have you? That's so sweet." Angie looked delighted.

"You certainly seem to have a way with him. I had a phone call from the children's center yesterday afternoon to say that the kids had a great time. Especially Felicity. Apparently, she's been raving about you and Comet. She's asked if they can all visit again today."

"Isn't that great?" Gina was delighted
that Fliss had enjoyed herself so much.
Helping someone discover a love for ponies
was the best feeling in the world.

"Yes, it is," Angie agreed. "I love to see
the kids and ponies together. But with an
extra visit, it means we have a really busy
day. There's a new pony arriving later. By
all accounts it's in pretty bad shape, so I'd
prefer any visitors to be out of the way
when it arrives."

"Oh, what a shame," Gina said, already
worried for the poor pony.

"Do you know if your mom's planning
on coming over?" Angie asked. "We really
could use some extra help today."

"She has to take the car into the garage
this morning—that's why I rode over
earlier. Maybe you could call her and ask if

she's coming here later?" Gina suggested.
"But I can stay and help. What do you
want me to do?"

"You're a star. Thanks, Gina. Could
you turn out the ponies into the paddock
for me and then help with mucking out?"

"No problem!" Gina said, already
crossing the stable.

She led Minky and Dancer out first,
watching as the little black-and-white
pony and the sturdy roan kicked up their
heels and cantered to the bottom of the
field. She then came back for Porter, the
beautiful ex–show jumper, before finally
leading Comet out.

"I'll see you later," she said to him
as she closed the paddock gate. "I loved
floating on that cloud with you. It was
fun, wasn't it?" she said fondly.

The magic pony's deep-violet eyes
gleamed affectionately. "Yes, it was. It
reminded me of cloud-racing with
Destiny."

Gina noticed a flicker of sadness cross
his face. "We'll go out looking again really
soon."

Comet brightened. "Thank you, Gina."
He turned and trotted toward Minky, who
was already munching on the sweet grass.

Gina thought about Comet's kindness to her as she finished mucking out. *He's the best friend anyone could have*, she said to herself.

She was determined to ride him properly the next time they went out searching for Destiny. Comet had been really good about them using the cloud, but they could do a better ground search if she rode him. Besides, she owed it to her special friend.

Gina was putting away her tools when Angie called across the yard to say that hot chocolate and food were ready in the farmhouse.

"I've spoken to your mom, and she's popping over later. She also said it looked as if you'd missed breakfast. So you're to get yourself over here, young lady.

Pronto!" Angie ordered, smiling.

"Yes, ma'am!" Gina called back, grinning.

Her tummy was rumbling like a freight train, and she realized she was starving. She pushed a strand of hair off her sweaty face and went to wash her hands. In the farmhouse kitchen, Angie and a couple of her staff were seated at a huge wooden table, eating a big breakfast. Gina joined them. Her toasted bacon sandwiches and mug of hot chocolate were delicious.

"Hot chocolate in the middle of summer?" Angie teased with a grin.

"Any time of year is hot-chocolate time!" Gina insisted, draining her mug.

The second Gina finished eating, she excused herself and went back outside to Comet. The minibus had just pulled up in the yard, and the caretakers and kids were getting out.

"Fliss is first off the bus," Gina told Comet. "She must be really eager to see you again."

"I am glad to see her, too!" Comet neighed, and twitched his tail as Fliss whirred toward him in her colorful wheelchair. Her caretaker, Jane, walked beside her.

"Hiya, Gina! Hiya, Comet!" Fliss wore a lemon tracksuit today, and there were purple bangles on her thin wrists.

"Hello, Gina," said Jane, smiling.

Gina greeted them warmly. "Hi, Jane. Hi, Fliss. Good to see you again." She thought the little girl looked even paler than the previous day. There were dark shadows beneath her eyes. But the moment she saw Comet, Fliss's face lit up. She reached up to pat his cheek, and Comet bent his head so Fliss could put her arms around his neck and give him a hug.

"You remember me, don't you, boy?" Fliss crooned, giving him a big wet kiss on his nose. She glanced at Gina, a look of determination on her small pinched face. "Okay. I've made up my mind! I want to ride him now—right now!"

Gina looked at Jane, who nodded.

"No problem. I'll help."

Looking back at Fliss, Gina grinned. "You're on!"

Chapter
SEVEN

"Feel okay up there?" Gina asked Fliss.
"Tell me if you want Comet to stop so
you can take a break, okay?"

"No chance!" Fliss cried.

Gina led Comet slowly around
the yard, with Fliss sitting in the bulky
western-style saddle, which supported her
small frame better than an English one.

"I'm *so* loving this!" Fliss said, beaming

from ear to ear as she clung tightly to the pommel at the front of the saddle. "I'm actually riding a pony! Yay!"

Comet was enjoying himself, too. He moved at a smooth, gentle pace and kept his head up high, so the little girl wouldn't fall if she slipped forward. But nothing happened and Fliss rode around the yard with a big grin on her face. "Look at me!" she called, waving to everyone she passed.

After the session, Jane helped Fliss dismount and get back in her wheelchair. As she settled down, Fliss seemed to sink with tiredness. But she still insisted on giving Comet a good-bye hug before she left. "See you again soon, Comet!" she said in a faint voice. "Bye, Gina. And thanks a bunch. I had a great time."

"Me too. I'm glad you enjoyed it,"
Gina said, a bit worried that Fliss seemed
so tired after such a short ride. She stood
beside Comet, waving as the minibus
drove away.

Angie came over as Gina was
unbuckling Comet's saddle. "I'm glad Fliss
had fun. She's got some good memories
to take with her when she goes into the
hospital."

"Hospital?" Gina exclaimed.

Angie nodded. "Jane told me she
has to have regular treatment for her

condition. Apparently Fliss is used to it,
but she gets very fed up with having to
stay in the hospital for a week at a time."

"Oh, what a shame," Gina said
sympathetically. That explained why Fliss
had looked unwell, although she had been
trying to hide it.

"Fliss is a brave girl. I like her," Comet
neighed as she removed his bridle.

"Me too," Gina agreed. "I hope
she'll be okay." She wished she could do
something to help. Maybe she'd ask her
mom if they could visit her in the hospital.

She unbuckled the western-style
saddle and put it away before coming out
of the tack room. "Time for some yummy
oats for you," she said to Comet.

Just then a jeep with a trailer pulled
into the yard. Shrill squeals and neighs

came from inside. There was a clang of hooves against the metal sides.

"That new pony doesn't sound good," Gina said. She was dying to go and peer over the trailer's back door and see what was making such a noise. "Do you mind waiting for your oats for a minute?" she asked Comet.

Comet shook his head, his ears swiveling toward the trailer. "I would like to wait here and see the new pony, too."

Gina watched anxiously as Angie and the jeep's driver unbolted and then let down the trailer's ramp. Cowering inside, her eyes rolling in fear, was the thinnest pony Gina had ever seen. The little mare was a lovely deep-chestnut color, with a flaxen mane and tail, and four white socks. Her mane and tail were tangled, and her

coat and feet were caked in mud.

"Oh, the poor thing," Gina said
breathlessly. "You can see all her ribs. She's
going to need lots of feeding and care."

The rescued pony whinnied and
kicked out again, pulling against the frayed
rope that tethered her, her ears twitching
crazily. Gina was frightened she'd hurt
herself against the trailer's sides.

Comet neighed softly and the other
pony froze in shock. Pricking up her
ears, she turned her head toward Comet

and listened to him with surprise. After
a moment, she gave a rather nervous
nicker of reply.

Comet nodded and then snorted
reassuringly. "She says her name is
Willow," he told Gina. "She doesn't trust
humans. She thinks they are all mean and
cruel."

"Oh, that's awful!" Gina's soft heart
went out to Willow, who was now
shivering and trembling with fear.

Gina immediately wanted to show
the pretty chestnut pony that not all
humans were horrible. But how did you
persuade such a scared pony that you
didn't mean her any harm?

Comet neighed again and Willow
listened more calmly. This time, when the
magic pony finished, Willow turned to

look at Gina. Her large dark eyes were
calmer now and her ears were pricking
forward in curiosity.

Gina couldn't believe the change in
the little chestnut. "What did you say to
her?" she whispered to Comet.

"She asked who you were. I told
her that you are a kind person, whom
she can trust." His violet eyes softened.

"Willow needs you, Gina."

Gina gulped as Comet's words sank deeply into her. It seemed like an impossible task, but she knew that she had to help this little chestnut mare. Looking up at Comet, she gave him a smile of total trust.

Angie took charge. "Right. Stand back, everyone. Time to get this pony into a nice clean stable." She moved toward the ramp and had barely put her foot on the bottom of it when Willow reared up in alarm and the frayed rope she was tied with snapped.

"Oh no! Steady there, girl," Angie said softly. "No one's going to hurt you."

But Willow wasn't listening. She snorted, squealed, and stamped, and tried to wheel around in the small space.

"Okay. I get the message," Angie said, backing away and stepping down. She drew a hand through her fair hair. "Poor little thing. She's terrified. We need to get her out of there before she really hurts herself. But I can't see her letting anyone near her."

Gina found herself walking over to the trailer. "She'll let me," she said confidently. "I'll try, Angie."

Angie shook her head. "No, Gina. Absolutely not. It's much too dangerous . . ."

Chapter
EIGHT

Gina felt a stir of dismay. She looked
at the terrified chestnut pony, cowering
in the corner of the trailer, and knew she
couldn't take no for an answer.

"*Please*, Angie. I'll be very careful," she
said in her most persuasive voice.

Angie frowned doubtfully. "I still don't
think it's a good idea—"

"You can watch me the whole time!"

Gina rushed on. "And I promise I won't go too close, until you tell me it's safe. Please, Angie," she said again. "I have to do this!"

"This means a lot to you, doesn't it?"

"Yes, it does."

Angie nodded slowly. "Well, all right. But go very slowly and don't take your eyes off her. And hightail it backward right away if I tell you to. Okay?"

"Deal," Gina agreed.

Despite her earlier confidence, her tummy clenched with nerves as she went over to stand beside Angie and looked up the ramp.

"Hello, girl," she said softly. "Don't be scared. I'm Gina and I want to be your friend. You're going to love it here." She kept her voice low. "This is a great place and everyone wants to make you better. Just give us a chance . . ."

Willow stood still, watching with wide eyes.

"So far, so good," Angie said approvingly. "You're doing fine."

Some instinct told Gina not to move up the ramp. "That's good. See? I'm not mean or scary," she said gently. "I'm just going to stand here."

Willow twitched her ears, as if to say, *Why are you waiting there?* Ducking her head, she lifted one dainty front leg. She took a small step forward. Twitching her matted tail, she took another step.

Now she had her front hooves on the ramp. She stood there calmly, a bit surprised at herself, and then looked up at Gina expectantly.

"Oh, so now you want me to show you your new stable, huh?" Gina waited patiently as Willow came slowly down the ramp. Gina resisted the urge to reach out, and stood with her hands behind her back.

Willow came close and sniffed her T-shirt and jeans, getting used to her scent.

After a few moments, Gina spoke gently again. "Ready now? Come on, then." She crossed her fingers, slowly turned, and took a few steps.

Willow stepped off the ramp and followed her.

Gina stopped, reached smoothly behind her, and took hold of the broken rope. "Here we go. Brave girl. You did really well," she crooned as she led the little mare into the stable, put her in her stall, and bolted the door.

"Good job, Gina," Angie congratulated Gina as she came back into the yard. "That was very impressive. You've got a real instinct for this work. How would you like to work with Willow? It will be a slow process, and you'll need a lot of patience. But she seems to trust you, and that's a big first step for a pony that's been treated so badly. What do you say?"

"I say yes. Yes, please!" Gina said, proud that Angie trusted her with such an important job. "Wait until I tell Com—I mean, er . . . Mom," she corrected herself quickly. "She won't believe it!"

She hurried over to where Comet was waiting and told him the news. "Isn't that fantastic? But I couldn't have done it without your help."

Comet nudged her arm affectionately. "I did not do very much. You helped Willow overcome her fear by staying calm and letting her come to you."

"Yeah, I guess I did!" Gina said. "It was really weird. I completely forgot to be nervous or scared, because I was too busy thinking about Willow."

Comet nodded wisely. "Sometimes we are braver than we think we are."

Over the next few days, Gina arrived at Horseland early every morning. She helped with mucking out stables, leading out and exercising the ponies, cleaning tack, and grooming. And there were always visitors to show around, and new ponies and horses arriving. She was making good progress with Willow.

The little chestnut mare now pricked her ears and stood calmly when Gina approached her stall.

The weekend dawned bright and clear when Gina's mom dropped her at Horseland on her way to the store. "Have fun. And say hi to Comet for me!"

"I will. Thanks for the lift!" Gina waved as her mom drove away.

She went straight into the stable to see Comet before she started work, as she always did. Two friendly whinnies rang out, and Gina did a double take.

"Did you hear that, Comet? Willow just said hello to me, too!"

Gina slowly reached up to stroke the chestnut mare's nose. Willow flicked her ears, but didn't shy away. She gave a long soft contented blow, as if to say *This place isn't too scary after all.*

"She's so pretty," Gina said as she looked into the mare's big dark eyes. "I think Willow and I are going to become good friends." Gina beamed at Comet.

Comet nodded. His violet eyes gleamed with satisfaction.

Later, Gina was brushing Comet's deep bay coat until it gleamed, when she heard Angie talking to one of the staff inside the tack room. ". . . such a shame. She was doing so well, until she found out she has to stay in the hospital longer. The doctor said she needs something to cheer her up."

"They're talking about Fliss!" Gina realized with a stab of guilt. She remembered that she had planned to visit the sick girl, but with Willow arriving, the thought had gone right out of her mind. She had an idea. "Comet! How about if we . . ."

The magic pony listened hard as she explained. "It is a good plan," he said. "Lead me to the bush at the bottom of the paddock, Gina."

Gina did so. All she could think about was poor lonely, unhappy Fliss. Well, she was about to get one huge surprise.

"Ready? Climb onto my back, Gina," Comet neighed, his eyes twinkling expectantly.

Gina took a deep breath. *I know I can do this*, she silently told herself. Fliss needed her and Comet. Before her courage failed her again, Gina climbed up, sat astride Comet, and wrapped her hands in his mane. "Let's go!" she urged, kicking him on.

A familiar prickling sensation flowed down her fingers as violet sparks ignited in Comet's bay coat, and tiny misty rainbows glimmered around him. He leaped forward and sped away.

Comet gave a neigh of triumph. "Well done, Gina. You are riding again!"

"Oh my goodness. I am!" Gina gasped in amazement. "Wow! I really am! And I'm not even a little scared!" She could hardly believe it. Riding the magic pony felt like the most natural thing in the world.

Comet's tail streamed out behind him as he galloped along invisibly. "You were too busy thinking about Fliss to feel scared. Just like with Willow. You did not need magic. Your own kindness has cured you!"

Gina realized that he was right. She could feel proud of herself for conquering her fear. And her reward was riding the most amazing pony in the universe!

Chapter
NINE

A surge of happiness glowed through
Gina from head to toe. She felt as if she
was filled with fizzy lemonade. Comet
was wonderful to ride, so fast and
smooth. His warm magic made her feel
safe, no matter how swiftly he weaved
past obstacles and dodged past anything
in their way.

She wanted to go on riding her

magical friend forever, and never stop!

Crouching over, Gina moved expertly in time to his powerful strides. She realized how much she had missed riding and knew that River would be glad she had worked through her fear. She promised herself that she'd go to visit the little gray pony in the animal park and tell her all about Comet.

"Wow! I love this so much! Go, Comet, go!" she cried.

As the hospital came into sight, Comet leaped into the air and his hooves carried them upward and over it in a mighty leap. A sprinkle of rainbow dust rained down, and in the center of it, Gina saw a small, pale little girl sitting in bed in a room next to the parking lot.

"There's Fliss!" she said, pointing.

"I see her." Comet landed in the parking lot, next to some bushes. Suddenly, he stopped and looked down at the ground.

Gina peered over his shoulder to see what he was looking at. Her eyes widened.

Stretching away across the hospital parking lot was a faint line of softly glowing violet hoofprints.

"Destiny has been here!" Comet told her.

Gina gasped. Did that mean he was leaving right now to go after his twin? "Is she somewhere nearby?" she asked anxiously.

"No, the trail is cold. But now I know that Destiny came this way. When I am closer to her, I will hear her hoofbeats."

"Will I be able to hear them?" Gina asked.

"Yes, if we are together. But other humans will not hear them. And I may have to leave suddenly, without saying good-bye, to catch up with Destiny," he said seriously.

Gina bit her lip. "Couldn't you and Destiny stay at Horseland?" she asked hopefully. "Then we could all be friends."

Comet shook his head. "I am afraid
that is not possible. We must return to
Rainbow Mist Island and our family. I
hope you understand, Gina."

Gina nodded sadly. She swallowed hard

and tried not to think about Comet leaving.

"Let's go and see Fliss now," she suggested, changing the subject.

She dismounted and they walked down a path at the side of the hospital building. Fliss lay on a bed in her room. She looked very tired and pale.

The window was open, and Gina tapped on it to get her attention.

Fliss frowned. As she turned and saw them, she did a double take. A huge smile spread over her face. "Comet? Gina? What are you doing here?"

"We came to see you," Gina said, smiling back. She opened the window a bit more, so that Comet could put his head inside the room.

Fliss laughed with delight. "Way to go, Comet! I bet that's the first time a pony's

been inside this hospital." She looked at
Gina, puzzled. "Did you get here in a
horse trailer or something?"

"Um . . . yeah, kind of," Gina said
evasively, only just realizing that she hadn't
thought about explanations. "But I . . . er,
borrowed Comet without Angie knowing,
so don't tell anyone. Or I'll be in big
trouble. Okay?"

"Cross my heart!" Fliss exclaimed. "I
can't believe this. It's so cool!"

"So—how are you?" Gina asked.

Fliss's cheeks were flushed as pink
as her favorite tracksuit. "I *was* totally
bored. But I'm not now. Tell me what's
happening at Horseland, and don't leave
anything out!"

"Well, a new pony arrived. She's called
Willow. You're going to love her . . ."

Gina held on tight as Comet galloped back toward Horseland. They swept along past houses, stores, and roads until they came to open countryside. Moments later, the old farmhouse came into view.

"That was great, Comet. We really cheered Fliss up, didn't we?"

Comet snorted in agreement. With a final surge and a sprinkle of violet glitter, he bounded into the paddock. Minky, Dancer, and Porter were already in there, nibbling the sweet grass and enjoying the sunshine.

And so was a little chestnut mare with a flaxen mane and tail, and four white socks.

"Willow!" Gina cried.

She was delighted to see the little

mare with the other ponies. Even after
just a few days, the change in Willow was
amazing. She had begun to put on weight,
and her coat was starting to shine. When
Willow saw Gina and Comet, she trotted
over to the fence.

Gina dismounted, and she and Comet

walked over to her. Willow huffed out
a warm breath and rubbed her chestnut
nose against his silky neck. Comet gently
nibbled her mane.

Gina smiled at them. They were so
sweet.

She looked at the stables, imagining all
the ponies in the future who would need
her help. And she knew what she wanted
to do for the rest of her life.

As she smiled at Comet, she felt like
the luckiest girl in the world.

It was unusually quiet, with no one
around. Gina guessed they were all in
the farmhouse having tea. Suddenly, she
heard a sound she'd been hoping for and
dreading at the same time.

The hollow sound of galloping hooves
overhead.

She froze. Destiny was here! There was
no mistake.

Comet flicked his tail and raced down
to the bottom of the paddock. Gina ran
after him and reached him just as there
was a bright flash and rainbow mist
swirled around him.

In the middle of it, Comet stood
there in his true form, no longer a
dark bay Dartmoor pony. Sunshine
gleamed on his noble arched neck, cream
coat, and flowing golden mane and
tail. Magnificent wings, covered with
gold feathers, spread upward from his
shoulders.

"Comet!" Gina gasped. She had
almost forgotten how beautiful he was.
"Are . . . are you leaving right now?"

His glowing violet eyes softened,
and sadness flickered across them for a
moment. "I must, if I am to catch Destiny
and take her home safely."

Gina's eyes stung with tears, and she
swallowed hard. She knew she must find
the courage to let her friend go. She ran
forward, threw her arms around his neck,

and laid her cheek against his silken coat.

"I'll never forget you," she whispered brokenly.

"You have been a good friend, Gina. I will not forget you, either." Comet allowed her to hug him one last time, then gently backed away. "Farewell. Ride well and true," he said in a deep musical neigh.

There was a final flash of violet light and a silent explosion of rainbow sparks that tinkled like fairy laughter as they touched the grass.

Comet spread his golden wings and soared upward. He faded and was gone.

Gina stood there, stunned by how fast everything had happened. Her throat ached with unshed tears. Something lay in the grass. It was a single glittering gold

wing feather. Bending down, she picked
it up.

The feather tingled against her hand
as it faded to a cream color. As Gina
slipped it into her pocket, she knew she
would always keep it to remind herself
of the magic pony and the amazing
adventure they had shared.

She turned sadly, about to walk back
up the paddock, and saw Willow waiting
at the fence for her. The little chestnut
pony reached out and very gently
touched her arm. *I'm still here. We'll look
after each other*, she seemed to be saying.

Gina's heart swelled, and a smile rose
up from deep within her as she knew
that Comet had made sure she had a new
pony friend for when he left her forever.
And with the magic pony's help, she had

rediscovered her love of riding.

"Thank you for being my friend, Comet," she whispered. "I hope you find Destiny and get back safely to Rainbow Mist Island."

About the
AUTHOR

Sue Bentley's books for children often include animals, fairies, and wildlife. She lives in Northampton, England, and enjoys reading, going to the movies, and watching the birds on the feeders outside her window. She loves horses, which she thinks are all completely magical. One of her favorite books is *Black Beauty*, which she must have read at least ten times. At school she was always getting told off for daydreaming, but she now knows that she was storing up ideas for when she became a writer. Sue has met and owned many animals, but the wild creatures in her life hold a special place in her heart.

Don't miss these Magic Ponies books!

Don't miss these Magic Kitten books!

#1 A Summer Spell

#2 Classroom Chaos

#3 Star Dreams

#4 Double Trouble

#5 Moonlight Mischief

#6 A Circus Wish

#7 Sparkling Steps

#8 A Glittering Gallop

#9 Seaside Mystery

A Christmas Surprise

Purrfect Sticker
and Activity Book

Starry Sticker
and Activity Book

Don't miss these Magic Puppy books!

Don't miss these Magic Bunny books!

#1 Chocolate Wishes

#2 Vacation Dreams

#3 A Splash of Magic